Animal
Pants

PUFFIN BOOKS

UK | USA | Canada | Ireland | Australia
India | New Zealand | South Africa

Puffin Books is part of the Penguin Random House group of companies
whose addresses can be found at global.penguinrandomhouse.com.

www.penguin.co.uk   www.puffin.co.uk   www.ladybird.co.uk

Penguin
Random House
UK

First published 2019
001

Printed in China
A CIP catalogue record for this book is available from the British Library

ISBN: 978–0–141–37834–3

All correspondence to:
Puffin Books, Penguin Random House Children's
80 Strand, London WC2R ORL

MIX
Paper from
responsible sources
FSC® C018179

Animal Pants

Giles Andreae
Nick Sharratt

PUFFIN

For Layla, with love - G.A.

For Janet - N.S.

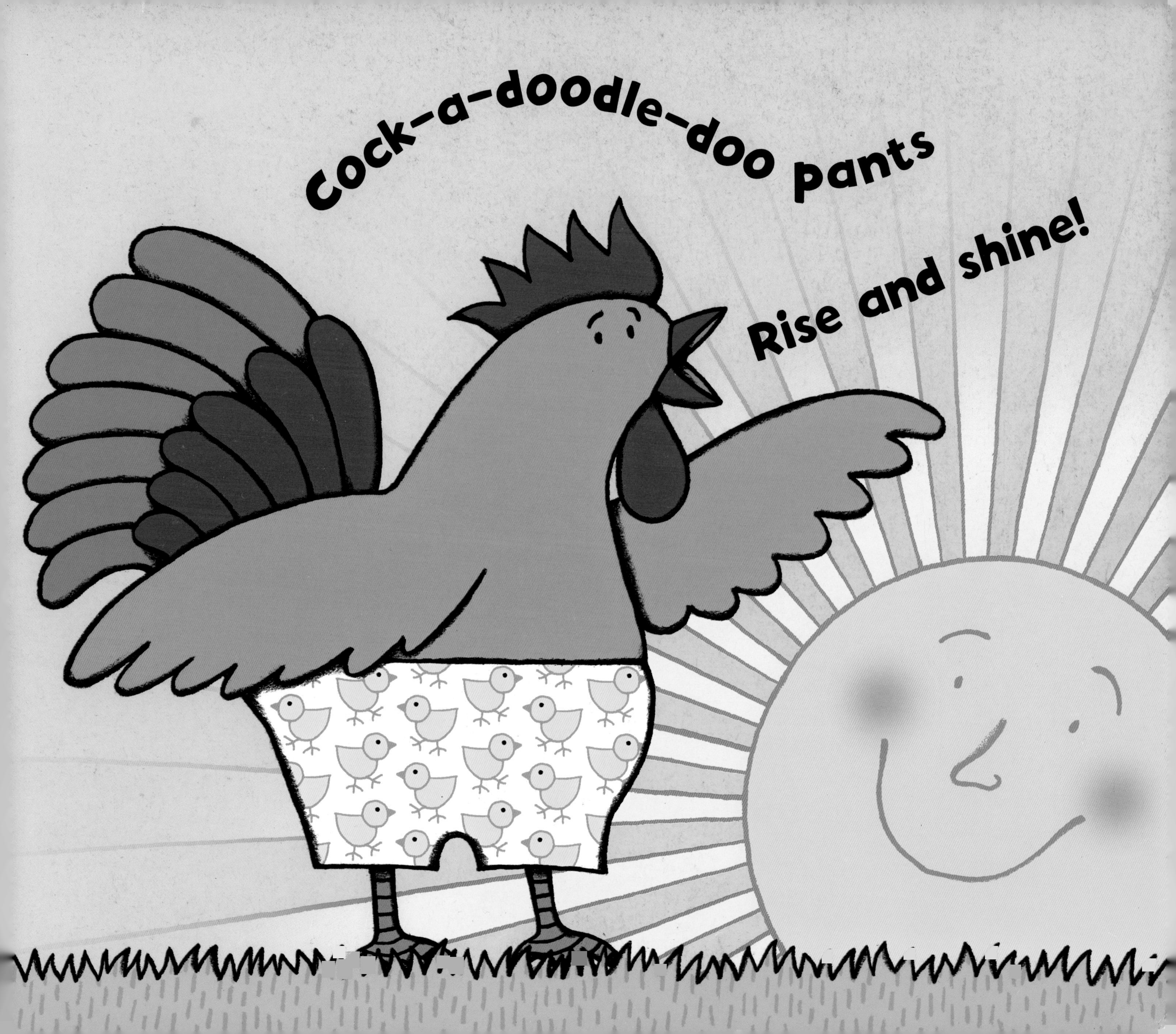

Cock-a-doodle-doo pants

Rise and shine!

Spiders sporting spotty pants

To cover up their botty pants

Big
and
tall
giraffe
pants

Pants for iguanas

And ravenous piranhas

Groovy pants for gibbons
With pictures of bananas

Ellie pants, smelly pants

Juggling in jelly pants

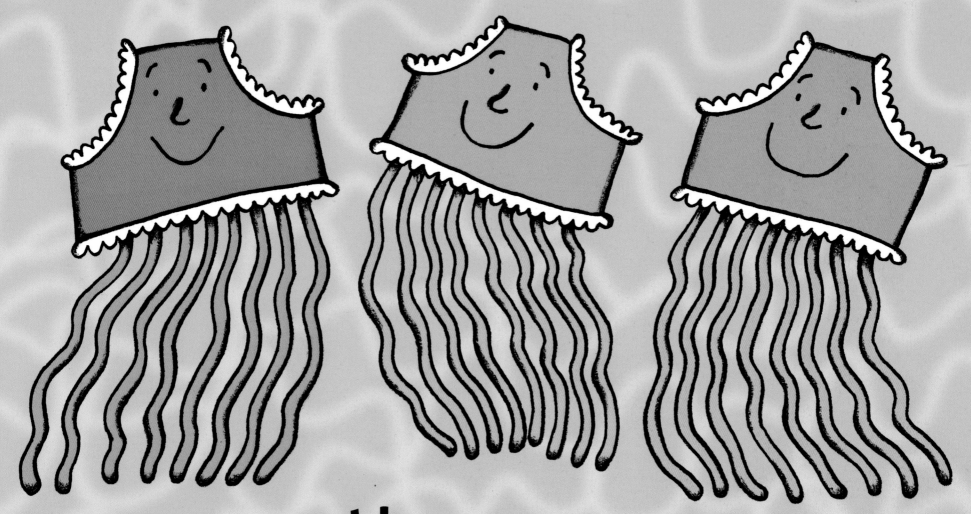

Wibble wobble woo!

Penguins' cold as ice pants

Narwhals' lucky dice pants

Pants for a cuddly polar bear

Curly-wurly poodle pants

Dachshunds
dressed in
doodle pants

whose pants would

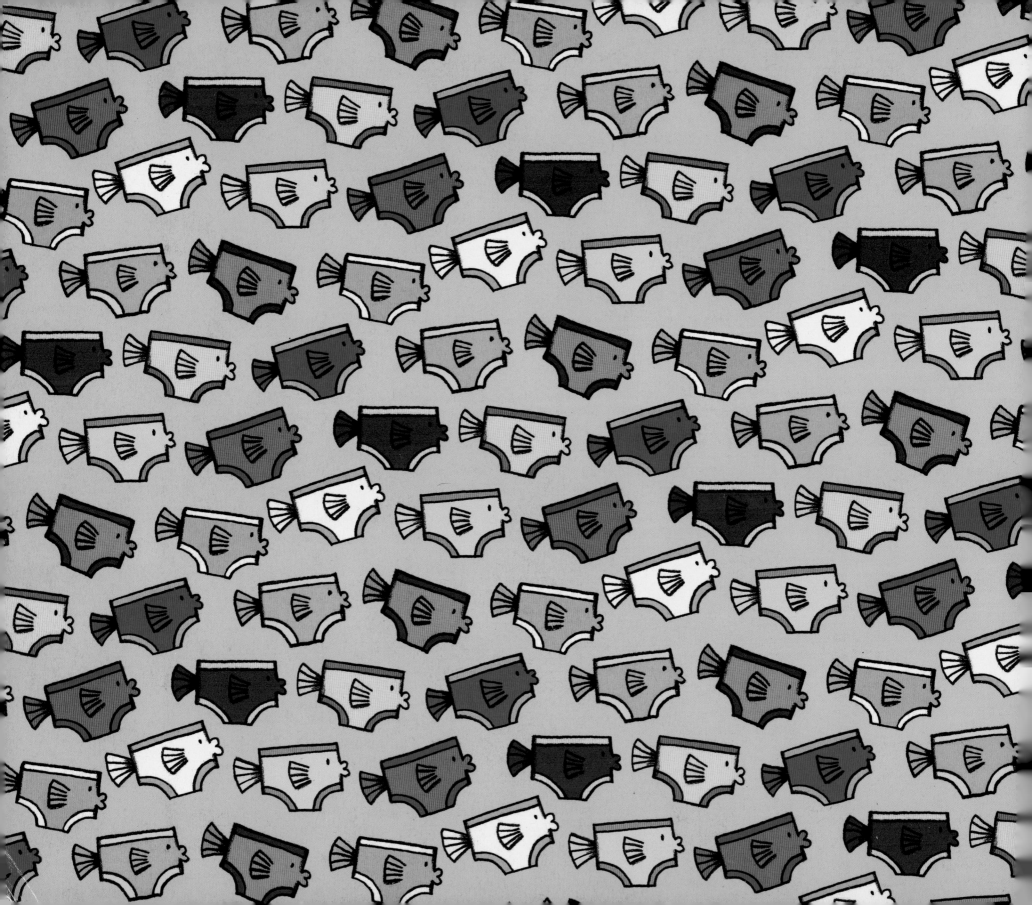

More books written by Giles Andreae

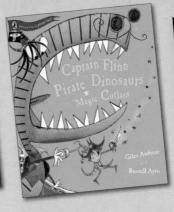

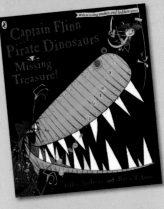

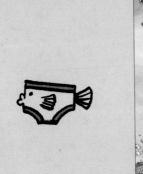

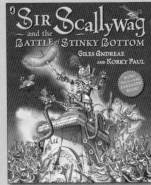

and illustrated by Nick Sharratt